North Dakota

South Dakota

Minnesota

Nebraska

Iowa

Wisconsin

Michigan

New York

New Hampshire

Vermont

Maine

Massachusetts

Rhode Island

Connecticut

New Jersey

Delaware

Maryland

Washington, D.C.

Kansas

Missouri

Illinois

Indiana

Ohio

Pennsylvania

West Virginia

Virginia

Oklahoma

Arkansas

Kentucky

Tennessee

North Carolina

Texas

Mississippi

Alabama

Georgia

South Carolina

Louisiana

Florida

N

W E

S

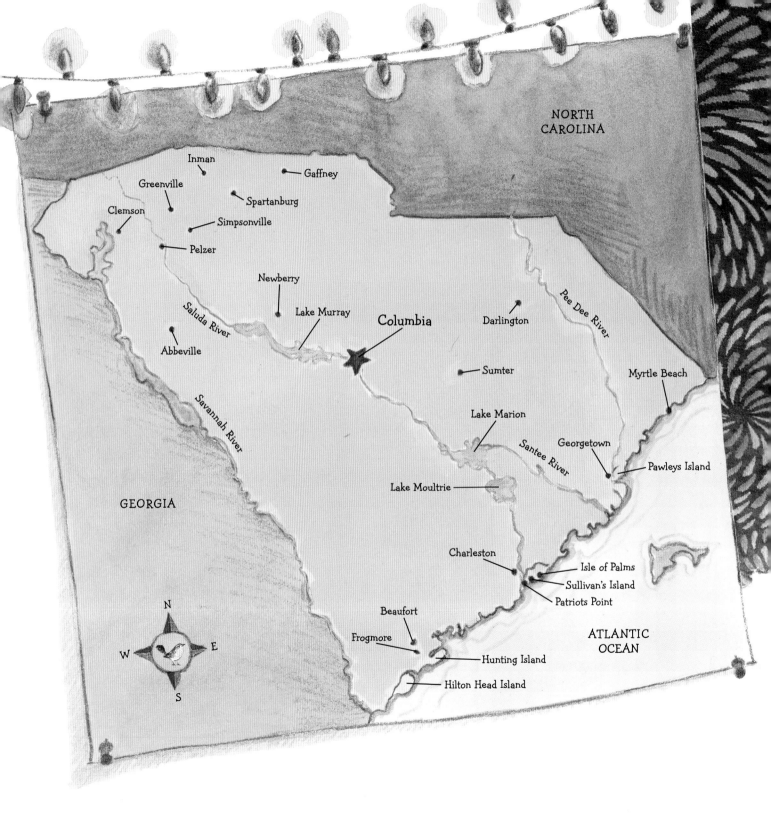

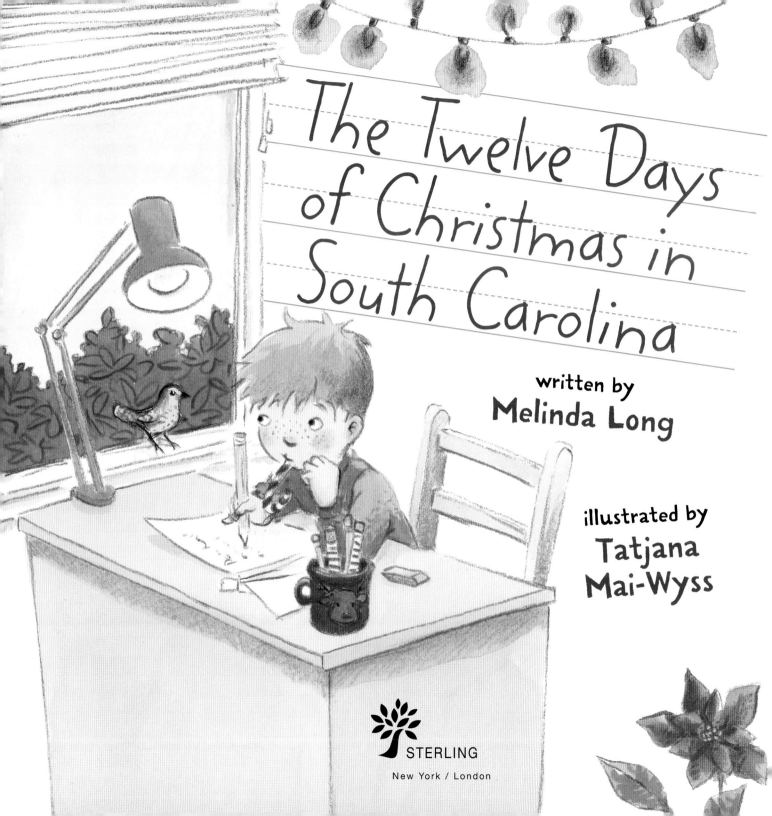

The Twelve Days of Christmas in South Carolina

written by
Melinda Long

illustrated by
Tatjana Mai-Wyss

STERLING

New York / London

Dear Laura,

I've been begging for months, and FINALLY my mama and daddy talked to your parents and they all decided that you can come to South Carolina to visit for Christmas vacation! I can't wait! By the time you get here, the festivities will be in full swing. Lights will be glowing and carolers will be singing. Mama will have a big pot of Frogmore Stew on the stove, and Daddy will be sizzling up some of his famous fried shrimp. You'll get to see my state at its holiday best, from the mountains to the sea.

Bring a warm coat because it can be really cold here in December. But you'd better also bring a few T-shirts because sometimes we get a blast of springtime early . . . nice and warm. Just <u>wait</u> until you see the presents I have for you—one for each of the twelve days of Christmas!

Love from your cousin,

Conner

P.S. This is an EXTRA-special place to celebrate Christmas because it's the home of Joel Poinsett. Does his name sound kinda familiar? He's the guy who brought the beautiful red Christmas flowers we now call poinsettias to the U.S. from Mexico in the late 1820s. It wouldn't be Christmas without them!

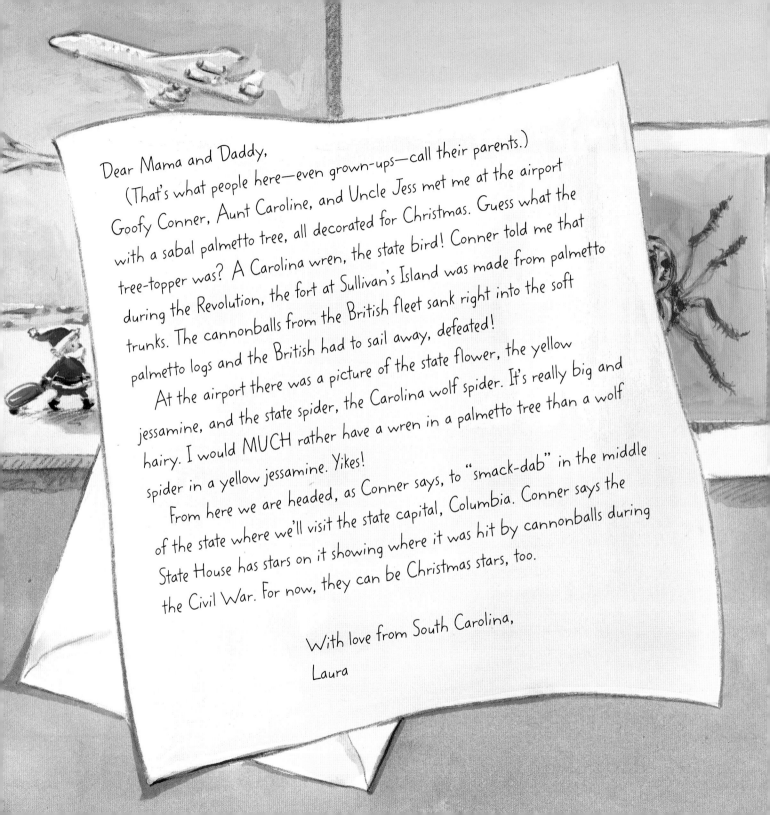

Dear Mama and Daddy,

(That's what people here—even grown-ups—call their parents.)

Goofy Conner, Aunt Caroline, and Uncle Jess met me at the airport with a sabal palmetto tree, all decorated for Christmas. Guess what the tree-topper was? A Carolina wren, the state bird! Conner told me that during the Revolution, the fort at Sullivan's Island was made from palmetto trunks. The cannonballs from the British fleet sank right into the soft palmetto logs and the British had to sail away, defeated!

At the airport there was a picture of the state flower, the yellow jessamine, and the state spider, the Carolina wolf spider. It's really big and hairy. I would MUCH rather have a wren in a palmetto tree than a wolf spider in a yellow jessamine. Yikes!

From here we are headed, as Conner says, to "smack-dab" in the middle of the state where we'll visit the state capital, Columbia. Conner says the State House has stars on it showing where it was hit by cannonballs during the Civil War. For now, they can be Christmas stars, too.

With love from South Carolina,

Laura

On the first day of Christmas,
my cousin gave to me . . .

a wren in a palmetto tree.

Dear Mama and Daddy,

Conner is a big history buff, so this morning we went straight to the State Museum in Columbia. South Carolina is just full of war heroes like Wade Hampton, a general for the South during the Civil War, and Robert Smalls, an African-American who escaped in a ship from South Carolina, fought for the North during the Civil War, and eventually became a state senator and helped write the South Carolina state constitution!

Thomas Sumter and Francis Marion, the Revolutionary War heroes, were my favorites. They both had awesome nicknames. Thomas Sumter was known as the "Gamecock" because he was an amazing fighter like the fierce gamecock roosters. Francis Marion was nicknamed the "Swamp Fox" because he hid with his troops in the swamps and attacked the British when they were least expecting it. Smart and sneaky! School's out for Christmas, but I'm still learning lots. Maybe I can be famous and have a cool nickname one day, like "The Lauranator" or "Laura, Video Game Champion of the World"!

Learning from the past in South Carolina,

Laura

On the second day of Christmas,
my cousin gave to me . . .

2 patriots

and a wren in a palmetto tree.

"From ghoulies and ghosties
And long-leggedy beasties
And things that go bump in the night,
Good Lord, deliver us!"

That's an old Scottish saying. It's kind of funny because the people here seem to LOVE talking about their ghosts. Georgetown and Charleston have plenty of "haints," but there are ghost stories all over the state. Tonight, Conner gave me my best Christmas surprise yet. He held a flashlight up to his face and told scary stories about a ghostly girl named Alice who searches for her lost engagement ring night after night, and one about a headless rider on a white horse. The one I liked the most was about the Gray Man of Pawleys Island. People here say he was killed trying to get home to his fiancée and came back later as a ghost to warn her of a hurricane. Now he appears to people on Pawleys Island before every hurricane. If you see the Gray Man, your home will be safe from the winds. AhhOOOOooooo!

Shaking in my shoes in South Carolina,

Laura

On the third day of Christmas,
my cousin gave to me . . .

3 pale ghosts

2 patriots,
and a wren in a palmetto tree.

Dear Mama and Daddy,

The weather here is so strange! It was nice and warm yesterday, but last night we got hit by a huge ice storm. I'm writing this letter by candlelight because the power is out. Brrrrr!

There are pretty icicles all over the power lines, and every leaf and blade of grass is covered in a little cocoon of ice. I've never seen anything like it! In a few days, though, it's going to be sixty-five degrees again. I have my T-shirt and flip-flops ready.

Aunt Caroline says that if you don't like the weather here . . . just wait a minute. South Carolina has four very different seasons. In the spring, it's warm and breezy. By summer, Conner says it'll be so hot and humid you could cook eggs on the sidewalk and drink the air. (Would you eat anything cooked on the sidewalk?) The leaves in the fall are brilliant yellows, reds, and oranges. In the winter, South Carolina doesn't get much snow, but Conner says that once in a while one of these huge ice storms will swoop in, causing people to lose power for days. It might be fun to live by candlelight for a few days—we can pretend we're camping out. But I wonder if I could live for a week without video games.

Chillin' in South Carolina,

Laura

On the fourth day of Christmas, my cousin gave to me . . .

4 icicles

3 pale ghosts, 2 patriots, and a wren in a palmetto tree.

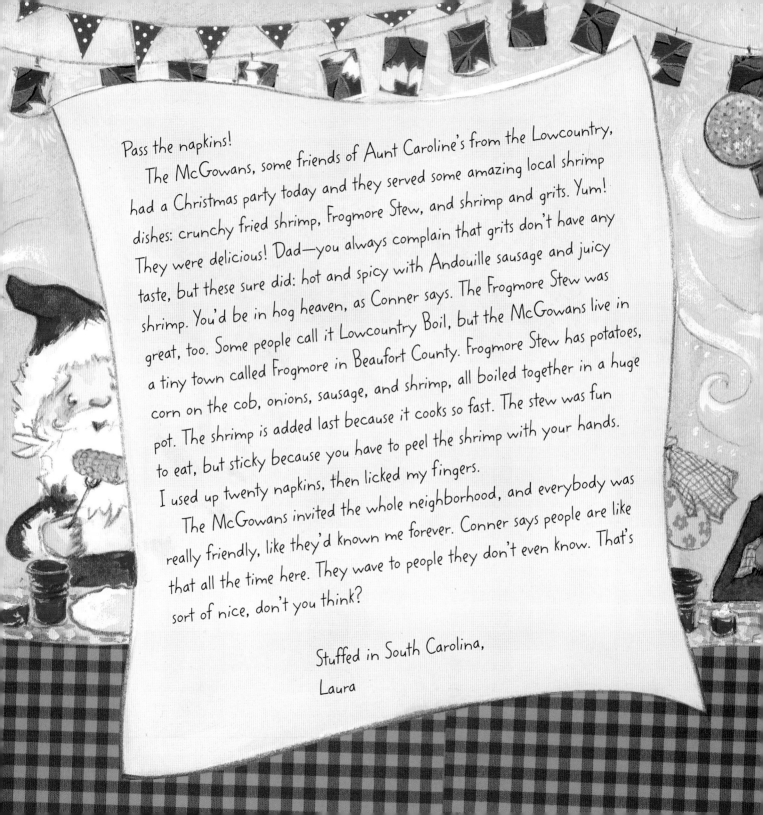

Pass the napkins!

The McGowans, some friends of Aunt Caroline's from the Lowcountry, had a Christmas party today and they served some amazing local shrimp dishes: crunchy fried shrimp, Frogmore Stew, and shrimp and grits. Yum! They were delicious! Dad—you always complain that grits don't have any taste, but these sure did: hot and spicy with Andouille sausage and juicy shrimp. You'd be in hog heaven, as Conner says. The Frogmore Stew was great, too. Some people call it Lowcountry Boil, but the McGowans live in a tiny town called Frogmore in Beaufort County. Frogmore Stew has potatoes, corn on the cob, onions, sausage, and shrimp, all boiled together in a huge pot. The shrimp is added last because it cooks so fast. The stew was fun to eat, but sticky because you have to peel the shrimp with your hands. I used up twenty napkins, then licked my fingers.

The McGowans invited the whole neighborhood, and everybody was really friendly, like they'd known me forever. Conner says people are like that all the time here. They wave to people they don't even know. That's sort of nice, don't you think?

Stuffed in South Carolina,

Laura

Ahoy thar, mateys!

Today we visited Charleston. We saw the ginormous Cooper River Bridge and the aquarium with its huge sharks. We also walked all over the aircraft carrier <u>Yorktown</u> at Patriots Point.

But my absolute favorite part of the day was finding out about the pirates. There are so many port towns on the coast of South Carolina that you hear about pirates everywhere. Did you know that the reason pirates called each other "scurvy dogs" was because they didn't get enough vitamin C and they got a nasty disease called scurvy? Pirates like Stede Bonnet, Blackbeard, Jack Rackham, and Mary Read all visited Charleston and the other ports. My favorite pirate was Anne Bonny. There weren't many female pirates because women were considered bad luck on a pirate ship. Anne was notorious before she ever became a pirate, but then she met "Calico Jack" Rackham and joined his crew wearing men's clothing. Shiver me timbers! She was a fierce fighter. Aargh and avast, me hearties! It's the pirate's life for me!

Swashbuckling in South Carolina,

Laura

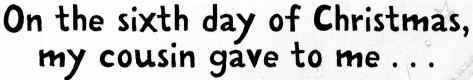

On the sixth day of Christmas, my cousin gave to me . . .

6 pirates prowling

5 golden shrimp, 4 icicles, 3 pale ghosts, 2 patriots, and a wren in a palmetto tree.

Dear Folks (they say that here, too),

Have you ever seen houses painted in rainbow colors all standing side by side? That's what Conner showed me today: Charleston's colorful Rainbow Row. The houses were built in the mid-1700s but weren't painted all those pinks, blues, and greens (also known as Colonial Caribbean colors) until later. Some people here say the houses were painted different colors so that sailors wouldn't have trouble finding the right boarding house late at night. Other people say the colors are there to deflect heat. It <u>does</u> get hot here, especially in the summer. I like the first story better. The houses sit near the Battery, looking out at all that beautiful water in the harbor. Can we paint my room in rainbow colors? I'll help!

Next, we went shopping outdoors at the Charleston Market. I bought a handmade shawl for you, Mom, with purple and yellow tassels on it, and a straw hat with a colorful band for you, Dad. I could have shopped there all day, but Uncle Jess said it was time to move on.

With love from colorful South Carolina,

Laura

On the seventh day of Christmas, my cousin gave to me . . .

7 rainbow houses

6 pirates prowling, 5 golden shrimp,
4 icicles, 3 pale ghosts, 2 patriots,
and a wren in a palmetto tree.

Quiet on the set!

Lights, camera, action! Did you know that two years ago Conner got to be an extra in a movie that was filmed right here in SC? No kidding. He went to the audition with some pictures of himself and they picked him out of a whole bunch of kids! We can watch the DVD when I get home. (Aunt Caroline and Uncle Jess gave me a copy of it for Christmas.) You can kind of see Conner in the crowd scene at the very beginning if you don't blink.

Today Conner took me to a real, live movie set and we collected autographs! Lots of movies have been filmed here, such as <u>The Big Chill</u>, <u>Forrest Gump</u>, <u>Leatherheads</u>, and a bunch more. Maybe the filmmakers like it here because there's a ton of great scenery of all different kinds to choose from. Maybe it's because the people are so nice and the food is so good. As Aunt Caroline says, "Well, bless their hearts!" Anyway, now I know I can be a movie star without moving to Hollywood! Do you want my autograph?

Becoming famous in South Carolina,

Laura

On the eighth day of Christmas,
my cousin gave to me . . .

8 actors acting

7 rainbow houses, 6 pirates prowling, 5 golden shrimp,
4 icicles, 3 pale ghosts, 2 patriots,
and a wren in a palmetto tree.

Dear Mom and Dad,

Where are my sunglasses? Wow, does this place have great beaches! You won't see too many surfers here because the waves aren't big, but the beaches are PERFECT for swimming and building sand castles—when the weather is warmer, that is. Myrtle Beach is like one big carnival. There are rides and souvenir shops everywhere and special shows at Christmastime. Other beaches, like Hunting Island and the Isle of Palms are quieter. You can walk on the beach at sunrise and collect beautiful shells. We watched dolphins leaping just offshore. Big show-offs! And at night, Conner says you can sometimes see baby turtles being born by the hundreds and flapping their tiny flippers to get to the ocean.

The state dance, the Shag, is something like the old jitterbug, but slower, and it is danced to the "beach music" of the Carolinas and Virginia. One of the really nice things about this state is that it's small enough that we could visit the mountains and the sea in just one day. Do you think we could come back here this summer?

With sand in my flip-flops,

Laura

On the ninth day of Christmas, my cousin gave to me . . .

9 dolphins leaping

8 actors acting, 7 rainbow houses, 6 pirates prowling,
5 golden shrimp, 4 icicles, 3 pale ghosts, 2 patriots,
and a wren in a palmetto tree.

Twinkle, twinkle, Mom and Dad,

The people in South Carolina just love their Christmas lights and I can see why. Everywhere you look, houses and trees are lit up with bright reds, blues, and yellows. It's so . . . sparkly. Aunt Caroline says that there are really great light displays all over the place, like the one at the Hollywild Animal Park in Inman and the Roper Mountain Science Center in Greenville, but tonight Conner gave me the funniest light display I've ever seen. In Pelzer, a little town in the Upstate, people in one neighborhood decorate their houses and THEMSELVES! They dress up in Christmas costumes covered in lights. Thousands of visitors drive through the neighborhood and the light people wave at all the cars as they slowly drive by. We stayed in line for an hour before we got to the light people. After all that time, I was dying to have one of those sparkly costumes for myself. (Aunt Caroline said to ask next time before we borrow the tree lights.)

Sparkling in South Carolina,
Laura

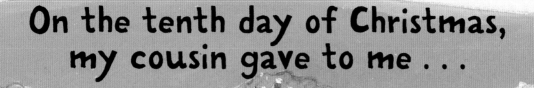

On the tenth day of Christmas,
my cousin gave to me . . .

10 sparkling people

9 dolphins leaping,
8 actors acting, 7 rainbow houses, 6 pirates prowling,
5 golden shrimp, 4 icicles, 3 pale ghosts, 2 patriots,
and a wren in a palmetto tree.

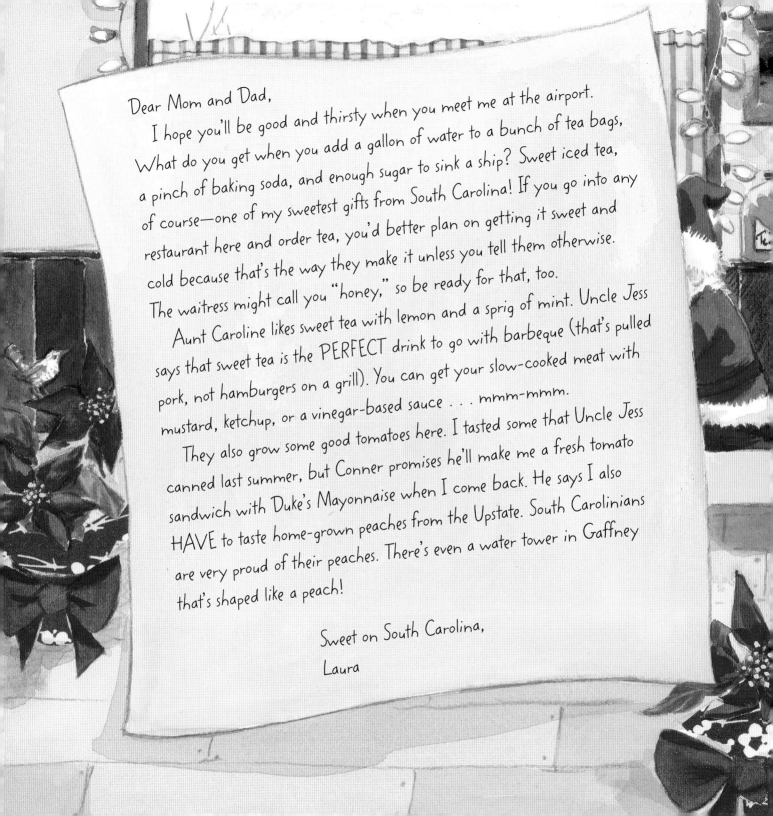

Dear Mom and Dad,

I hope you'll be good and thirsty when you meet me at the airport. What do you get when you add a gallon of water to a bunch of tea bags, a pinch of baking soda, and enough sugar to sink a ship? Sweet iced tea, of course—one of my sweetest gifts from South Carolina! If you go into any restaurant here and order tea, you'd better plan on getting it sweet and cold because that's the way they make it unless you tell them otherwise. The waitress might call you "honey," so be ready for that, too.

Aunt Caroline likes sweet tea with lemon and a sprig of mint. Uncle Jess says that sweet tea is the PERFECT drink to go with barbeque (that's pulled pork, not hamburgers on a grill). You can get your slow-cooked meat with mustard, ketchup, or a vinegar-based sauce . . . mmm-mmm.

They also grow some good tomatoes here. I tasted some that Uncle Jess canned last summer, but Conner promises he'll make me a fresh tomato sandwich with Duke's Mayonnaise when I come back. He says I also HAVE to taste home-grown peaches from the Upstate. South Carolinians are very proud of their peaches. There's even a water tower in Gaffney that's shaped like a peach!

Sweet on South Carolina,

Laura

On the eleventh day of Christmas,
my cousin gave to me . . .

11 jugs of sweet tea

10 sparkling people, 9 dolphins leaping,
8 actors acting, 7 rainbow houses, 6 pirates prowling,
5 golden shrimp, 4 icicles, 3 pale ghosts, 2 patriots,
and a wren in a palmetto tree.

Beware the kudzu monsters!

Conner gave me a whole field of them today. He says they're kudzu vines that covered everything that stood still last summer. Kudzu was brought to the South to stop the soil from washing away but it did the job TOO well. Now, kudzu grows wild, making everything it covers into big, leafy monsters. Since it seems unstoppable, people have found clever ways to use it. There are baskets, tea, paper, jelly, quiche, and hay made from kudzu. One day there may even be kudzu medicines, and everyone will be glad that they didn't get rid of it entirely.

Since the kudzu is all dried up now, there's room to use the field for football, which is <u>big</u> here! Other sports are, too. Joe Frazier, the heavyweight boxing champion, and Althea Gibson, the famous tennis champion, were from SC. We even saw the statue in Greenville of Shoeless Joe Jackson. He got his name by running the bases during a game in only his sock feet. Since Conner is a huge fan, we stopped by to leave a baseball on Shoeless Joe's grave, also in Greenville. Remember to bring a really BIG truck when you pick me up at the airport tomorrow!

Missing South Carolina already,
Laura

On the twelfth day of Christmas, my cousin gave to me . . .

12 kudzu monsters

11 jugs of sweet tea, **10** sparkling people, **9** dolphins leaping,
8 actors acting, **7** rainbow houses, **6** pirates prowling,
5 golden shrimp, **4** icicles, **3** pale ghosts, **2** patriots,
and a wren in a palmetto tree.

South Carolina: The Palmetto State

State Bird: the Carolina wren • **State Reptile:** the loggerhead turtle • **State Spider:** the Carolina wolf spider • **State Flower:** the yellow jessamine • **State Tree:** the sabal palmetto • **State Fruit:** the peach • **State Beverage:** milk • **State Gemstone:** the amethyst • **State Songs:** "Carolina" and "South Carolina on My Mind" • **State Dance:** the Shag • **State Music:** the spiritual • **State Mottos:** "Prepared in mind and resources" and "While I Breathe, I Hope."

Some Famous South Carolinians:

Mary McLeod Bethune (1875–1955), born near Mayesville, was an educator and civil rights leader who saw a great need for the education of African-American girls. She established the Daytona Literary and Industrial School for Training Negro Girls, which later became Bethune-Cookman College. Mary also founded The National Council of Negro Women.

James Brown (1933–2006), born in Barnwell, was a singer, songwriter, bandleader and dancer known as "the Godfather of Soul," "the hardest-working man in show business," and "Soul Brother Number One." James Brown is best known for songs such as "I Got You (I Feel Good)," and "Papa's Got a Brand New Bag."

Pat Conroy (1945–) has lived for many years in the Lowcountry of South Carolina. He is a best-selling novelist, famous for his books *The Prince of Tides*, *Beach Music*, and many others.

Jesse Jackson (1941–) was born in Greenville and is best known as a civil rights leader and a politician. In 1984 and 1988, he ran for presidential nomination. He founded the Rainbow Coalition.

Andie MacDowell (1958–), born in Gaffney, is a famous actress, star of *Groundhog Day*, *Barnyard*, and many other movies. She is well-known for her beautiful South Carolina accent.

Dori Sanders (1934–) was born in Filbert, the daughter of a sharecropper with nine brothers and sisters. She still runs her family peach farm, and is also the acclaimed writer of *Clover* and *Her Own Place*.

Joanne Woodward (1930–) is an Academy Award®–winning actress known for her many movie roles, including *The Three Faces of Eve*. She attended Greenville High School and began her acting career at Greenville Little Theatre.

To Thom, my loving husband, who knows everything about South Carolina.
A big THANKS to dedicated booksellers everywhere,
and all my F/B friends who have a great love for this beautiful state.
—M.L.

To my friends and family, who make South Carolina "home" for me.
—T.M.W.

STERLING and the distinctive Sterling logo are registered trademarks of Sterling Publishing Co., Inc.

Library of Congress Cataloging-in-Publication Data
Long, Melinda.
The twelve days of Christmas in South Carolina / written by Melinda Long ; illustrated by Tatjana Mai-Wyss.   p. cm.
Summary: Laura writes a letter home each of the twelve days she spends exploring South Carolina at Christmastime,
as her cousin Conner shows her everything from a wren in a palmetto tree to twelve kudzu vines.
Includes facts about South Carolina.
ISBN 978-1-4027-6672-5
[1. South Carolina--Fiction. 2. Christmas--Fiction. 3. Cousins--Fiction. 4. Letters--Fiction.] I. Mai-Wyss, Tatjana, 1972- ill. II. Title.
PZ7.L856Tw 2010
[E]--dc22   2009013957

Lot#:
4 6 8 10 9 7 5 3
07/12

Published by Sterling Publishing Co., Inc.
387 Park Avenue South, New York, NY 10016
Text © 2010 by Melinda Long
Illustrations © 2010 by Tatjana Mai-Wyss
The original illustrations for this book were created in watercolor,
colored pencils, and collage on watercolor paper.
Distributed in Canada by Sterling Publishing
c/o Canadian Manda Group, 165 Dufferin Street
Toronto, Ontario, Canada M6K 3H6
Distributed in the United Kingdom by GMC Distribution Services
Castle Place, 166 High Street, Lewes, East Sussex, England BN7 1XU
Distributed in Australia by Capricorn Link (Australia) Pty. Ltd.

The Academy Awards ® are a registered trademark of the
Academy of Motion Picture Arts and Sciences Corporation. All rights reserved.

Sterling ISBN 978-1-4027-6672-5

For information about custom editions, special sales, premium and corporate purchases, please contact
Sterling Special Sales Department at 800-805-5489 or specialsales@sterlingpublishing.com.

Designed by Kate Moll

CANADA

Washington

Montana

Oregon

Idaho

Wyoming

Nevada

Utah

Colorado

California

Arizona

New Mexico

Alaska

Hawaii

(NOT TO SCALE)

MEXICO